# FIRST LOVE, LAST LOVE

*A Work of Dramatic Verse by*

Edward Eaton

Published by
Dragonfly Publishing, Inc.

# FIRST LOVE, LAST LOVE

Paperback Edition
EAN 978-1-941278-86-4 | ISBN 1-941278-86-8

Hardback Edition
EAN 978-1-941278-87-1 | ISBN 1-941278-87-6

eBook Edition
EAN 978-1-941278-88-8 | ISBN 1-941278-88-4

Story Text Copyright ©2021 Edward Eaton
Cover Art & Illustrations Copyright ©2021 Terri Branson
Dragonfly Logo Copyright ©2001 Terri Branson

Published in the United States of America by
Dragonfly Publishing, Inc.
Website: www.dragonflypubs.com

# Dramatis Personae

| | |
|---|---|
| SNOWY | A stuffed bunny |
| RECTOR | A stuffed dog |
| GEORGE | A stuffed monkey |
| COUNT | A stuffed vampire |
| BABS | A fashion doll |
| JOE | An action figure |
| DANNY | An old man |
| BEAR | A stuffed bear |

\* \* \* \* \*

## A NOTE ON SET:

The action of the play is set in the television room of the house in which Danny grew up. The room has been partially converted into a sick room.

## A NOTE ON AGE:

DANNY is written and intended to be played as someone older (60+). There will be references to his age. Of course, readers and directors may see him as younger. The playwright has no objection to that sort of decision. As for the toys, the playwright sees them as being portrayed by adult actors. In fact, he sees them as being played by actors in their twenties — impossibly old in the eyes of a child. Other than BABS and JOE, the ages are not really important and can be left up to the imaginations of readers and the interpretations of directors. Even in the cases of BABS and JOE, an argument could be made for them to be older (though probably not very young). Toys may gather dust in a box, but do they age?

## A NOTE ON GENDER:

Some of the characters were conceived as being 'male'. Some of the words reflect that. Other characters have 'masculine' pronouns attached them — that was simply because pronouns were required in some cases. The playwright has not focused on 'masculine' or 'feminine' qualities, except in a couple of cases. The playwright allows that directors and readers might want to imagine the characters as the opposite gender (or no gender, as a stuffed Bunny has few if any 'male' or 'female' markers) and will take nor personal nor professional issue with those decisions nor with appropriate pronoun (or even word) changes (as long as they scan).

## A NOTE ON ACTS:

The play is written in three acts. There is no need for an intermission (in which case, cut the repeated lines from Act II in Act III). If there is an intermission, it should be placed between II and III.

# *Dedication*

To my wife, Silviya, and my son, Christopher.

*Sine quibus non*

Special thanks to Marcelline Block for her help with my atrocious French and to the Needham Community Theatre for their faith which resulted in the digital streaming production of the play in October of 2020.

# ACT I
## SCENE 1

*SNOWY, a stuffed bunny, enters with RECTOR, a stuffed dog.*

SNOWY
Wait. For the others.
I pray they will come. They know
Not the way. Show them.

Perhaps I am wrong.
Have I taken the wrong path?
Do I know this place?

There's an irony:
To have dared the journey, braved
The stairs, only to
Sojourn in the wrong
Room. It smells right, but feels wrong.
Or the opposite.

But we made the trek.
I must wait, or we'll be lost.

Wait without, Rector!

*Exit RECTOR.*

This must be it, for
This is the place that drew me,
The place that called me.

It has been so long.
Is my memory so good
After all these years?

For so long have we
Been kept in tight boxes 'neath
Boxes, hidden in
The damp recesses
Of a cold dungeon — Dungeon.
Yes, so I call it —
That much is forgot
Or blurred by damp time of our
Glorious yet brief
Lives in these rooms, in
This house, our victories and,
Yes, e'en our defeats.
But they were before
We found ourselves sentenced...damned
To coldness below.

At first I cried. I.
To be stuffed beside dusty
Plates, inside fragile
Bowls. Wrapped in paper.
Once we reigned in this place, if
This is the place. We
Lived and laughed and loved.
No room was forbidden us.
We sailed mighty ships.
We raced in fast cars.
We waged glorious battles.
Oh, how the walls and
Floors echoed with our
Cries. Great wars fought and refought.

Great, mysterious
Adventures filled our
Nights and our days. Tragedies
On every step.
Heroes behind each
Door. Bravery. Cowardice.

Yes, even romance.

Ah, romance! Awkward,
It was romance none-the-less.
That was not my forte.
Yet, I bore growing
Pangs as best I could.

    One day,
I lay nestled and
Warm among the sheets
And gamboled on the carpets.

The next, I and my
Kith found ourselves on
The shelves.

    The swords and the wands
That once were strewn 'cross
The floor became bats
And balls. The castles and ships
That were ever our
Scenery became
Athletes and models.

Then our
Adventures finished.
It was not long 'til
Alien, unloving hands
Shook the dust from our
Fur and used us as
Padding for forgotten and
Unwanted knick-knacks.

Once proud, once fierce, I…
Nay, we — for I was never
Alone — were consigned

To cardboard coffins
In a neglected corner
Of a neglected
Basement.

How many
Nights and days have we lain there?

A thousand days? A
Thousand thousand nights?

I cannot know. Dare not know.
Such numbers beyond
My skills, my knowledge.
I am not time's accountant.
I'm but his victim.

So many nights, to
Lie in our hellish prison
And hear the new lives
Cry out and laugh, play

Mere feet above us. New toys.
New adventures. New
Quests. Yes, even new
Children. New generations
Taking our domains.

We waited. Waited
For someone to come for us.
We cried out, "Here we
Are! Bring us back. This
Is our home. We know this place!

"Did we not scale the
Great staircase, suffer
The vast deserted wastelands
Of the living room?

"Did we not brave the
Terrible furnace of the
Kitchen?

    "Did I...yes
I, not once spend three
Days imprisoned in a dark
And lonely closet?

"We wandered through this
Place — our place, our home — suff'ring
Through illness, drying
Tears with our bodies.
We were ever ready with
A kiss, an embrace.

"Do we have no rights?

"Can we be denied our home?"

What comfort's a box
When just above us
A vast and infinitely
Varied world awaits?

Where is the comfort
In knowing, feeling, that friends
Are merely inches
From us, but denied
Our companionship?

    Boxes.
Boxes placed upon
Boxes — vaulting tow'rs
Of boxes reaching to the
Ceiling and sealed closed.

How many sobs have
I heard? Some ancient murm'rings
That drift like echoes

From a time long gone.
New cries.

    New generations
Of boxes piled on
Ours, crushing us 'neath
A new age's detritus —
Tomorrow's garbage.

Yet worse — the recent

Indignity. The boxes,
Our friends, are removed.
Taken away to
A place called 'The Dumps', there to
Be mulched, recycled.
Carted to thrift shops
And there left to gather dust
With strange, alien
Junk. Or to be dragged
Out and sold at garage sales.

My love, my past, my
Adventures, my pow'rs,
Beyond compare and precious:
They now have a price.

I'm worth fifty cents.
Twenty five, with the ashtray
Painstakingly wrought
By a loving child
And so praised for its beauty,
Sold as a key bowl
To a stranger with
A pick up, three children, two
Dogs, a bitter wife.

Am I to be chewed
By the dogs? Torn by the kids?
Again...be forgot?

This I cannot, will
Not suffer. My fate will not
Be dust and darkness.

I care not which of
My kind dares follow me. I
Will take back my home!

I will fight! I'll rage
And bring down the walls ere I
Allow myself to
Be discarded so!
This is my home as much as
Anyone else's.

Have I not this right?
Am I not so owed? Here, I'll
Live, laugh, love...e'en end.

If I must go on
Alone, then alone I'll be.
If with friends, then so.

> *He hears something.*

There is noise without.
Who comes?

    Rector?

    Nothing.

    P'rhaps
He's lost, or worse: caught.

I'll not be taken
By the foul woman in white
And sent back below.

P'rhaps it is my friends.
I can't know until they come.

What's Snowy to do?

Alone, I am weak.
But I am clever. I must
Know. To this end, I
Will listen, will learn
Who's friend, who's foe.

    To know, I
Must secrete myself.

*He does.*

\* \* \* \* \*

# ACT I
## SCENE 2

*Enter RECTOR and COUNT, a stuffed vampire.*

RECTOR

Where is bunny?

COUNT

Hush.

RECTOR

Where is bunny? Rector is
Asking. Don't hush me.

COUNT

I say, 'hush'. You do
Not know who or what lurks in
These shadows.

RECTOR

Nothing
Is lurking. I am
Trusting my nose.

Is strange smell
This room is having.

COUNT

P'rhaps your nose is old
And tired.

That was a long climb.

RECTOR
Not long for Rector.

Perhaps you are old.

COUNT
Had I fed, I would have flown.

RECTOR
Flown? You are not bird.

COUNT
I am a vampire.
I am weak for lack of blood,
But strong, I can fly.

Where are the rest, dog?

RECTOR
I prefer you call me 'hound'.

COUNT
Where are the rest...pup?

RECTOR
We left the ancient
One below. Climb was too high.

SNOWY
(aside)
That ancient mangy
One is no great loss
To our current purpose, but
What of the others?

RECTOR
The pair got lost near
Kitchen. She said she was chef.

SNOWY
(aside)
And astronaut and
CEO. There is
Nothing she cannot do, if
We believe her words.

COUNT
And so he followed
Her.

RECTOR
Of course, he is a man.

COUNT
I am a man as
Well, but I did not
Follow.

RECTOR
Why would you follow?
You have not woman.

COUNT
If I had that one
I would feed on her and then
I would have great strength.

Perhaps when she comes
I will smite down her man and
Take her for my feast.

RECTOR
She'll rip your fangs out.

COUNT
I am vampire. I fear none.

RECTOR
There is noise! She's here!

COUNT
Quickly, we must hide.

RECTOR
Is too late. The door opens.

COUNT
Oh, what shall we do?

RECTOR
Face our doom!

COUNT
It was
Rector —

RECTOR
What?

COUNT
It was Rector
Dared to threaten you.

RECTOR
I never! Count, you
Coward!

COUNT
Coward?!

RECTOR
Shh! She'll hear.

COUNT
The treachery is
Rector's!

RECTOR
Foul liar!

*Enter GEORGE, a stuffed monkey.*

Oh. It's you.

GEORGE
It's I.

RECTOR
We thought —

GEORGE

Hush

COUNT

Rector said —

GEORGE

Hush!

I need calm to think.
E'en your breathing annoys me,
But I'll suffer that
If you'll leave me be.

COUNT

Leave him be! He needs to think!

RECTOR

I said naught.

GEORGE

Quiet!

COUNT

He needs quiet, so
He can think, Do you hear me?

RECTOR

I'm not talking.

COUNT

Yet
You keep making noise.

I need a newspaper to
Smack him on the nose.

                RECTOR
You'll do no such thing.

                COUNT
Will too.

                RECTOR
Will not.

                COUNT
Will too.

                GEORGE
Guys.

                COUNT
You're interrupting.

                RECTOR
You're the one who keeps
Talking.

                COUNT
Quiet, dog!

                RECTOR
I am
Russian Wolfhound.

                GEORGE
Guys.

COUNT
You are not Russian
Wolfhound. You are nor Russian
Nor wolf, nor e'en hound.

RECTOR
Not Russian!?

COUNT
No. Not.

RECTOR
Oh, infamy! Why do you
Think I talk this way?

COUNT
Because you're stupid.

RECTOR
Why, I oughta....

COUNT
What?

RECTOR
What?

COUNT
What
Oughta you to do?

RECTOR
I...oughta...do...

GEORGE
Guys.

RECTOR
...Something.

COUNT
Something?

RECTOR
Yes...something.

COUNT
Then...I'll...do...something...
Too.

GEORGE
Guys.

RECTOR
No, you won't.

COUNT
Will too.

RECTOR
Nuh huh.

COUNT
Uh huh.

GEORGE
Guys!
Will you be quiet?

COUNT
I will suck your blood.

RECTOR
Nuh huh.

COUNT
Uh, huh.

RECTOR
I don't have
Blood. I've fluff inside

COUNT
Not fluff, but sawdust.

RECTOR
Say not so! Say not so!

GEORGE
Guys.

COUNT
Sawdust.

RECTOR
Ah!

COUNT
And mold.

RECTOR
Oh!

COUNT
And rot.

RECTOR
Oh, no!

COUNT
And pebbles.

RECTOR
No!

GEORGE
Guys.

COUNT
Insects
That crawl inside you.

GEORGE
Guys.

RECTOR
Oh! Oh!

COUNT
Crawling.
Eating away at your soul!

RECTOR
I howl! I rave!

GEORGE
Guys.

COUNT
They're inside you. They
Grow. They breed. They multiply,
And then they, they die!

RECTOR
Say it's not so.

GEORGE
Guys.

COUNT
Is so.

RECTOR
You lie.

COUNT
I speak truth.

GEORGE
Will you two shut up?

RECTOR
He is being mean.

GEORGE
I'm trying to think.

COUNT
It's not
Mean if it is true.

RECTOR
George —

GEORGE
I'm trying to
Monologue.

COUNT
Shh! He's trying
To monologue.

GEORGE
Thanks.

RECTOR
Should we go somewhere
Else?

GEORGE
That's not necessary.

RECTOR
You're monologuing.
Don't you need to be
Alone?

COUNT
That's 'soliloquy',
Not 'monologue'.

RECTOR
Oh.

Go ahead, George

GEORGE
Thanks.

RECTOR
We'll be quiet.

GEORGE
Okay.

RECTOR
So
You can monologue.

*Pause.*

Count?

COUNT
What?

RECTOR
Why does he
Not speak?

COUNT
I don't know.

George?

GEORGE
What?

COUNT
Why do you not speak?

GEORGE
I lost my train of
Thought.

RECTOR
Hee! Hee! He forgot his
Line.

GEORGE
I did not. I
Lost my train of thought.

COUNT
There's a difference there.

RECTOR
What
Do you want to say?

GEORGE
I need a first phrase.
Let me think.

*They think.*

RECTOR
I've got one! "The
Wrath of George I sing!"

That's because George is
Always so angry.

GEORGE
  I'm not.
Now shut the hell up!

COUNT
Nailed it, Rector.

RECTOR
  Yep.

COUNT
Ooh! Why not: "Of George's first
Disobedience
And the fruit of that —

GEORGE
No!

RECTOR
  I've got it! "To be or
Not to be — that is
George's question."

GEORGE
  No.

COUNT
Sounds good to me.

RECTOR
  Better in
The original.

GEORGE
Don't go there, Rector.

RECTOR
"taH pagh taHbe!"

COUNT
He went there.

RECTOR
Ouch! You hit me!

GEORGE
Did
Not.

RECTOR
Did too.

GEORGE
Well, you
Deserved it. I need to think.

RECTOR
We're trying to help.

GEORGE
Help by shutting up.

RECTOR
That's not nice.

COUNT
George, tell us why
You came upstairs now.

RECTOR
Easy. He followed
Snowy.

GEORGE
I did not follow
Snowy.

RECTOR
Snowy came
Up. You came after
Him. Ergo, you followed him.

GEORGE
Okay. I followed
Him. But I did not
Follow him.

RECTOR
I don't get it.
Anyway, Snowy
Is the boss.

COUNT
Oh, God.

GEORGE
Snowy is not the boss.

RECTOR
He
Was elected boss.

COUNT
I voted for you,
George.

RECTOR
Yet Snowy was chosen.

GEORGE
Yes, and there's the rub.

Why did Snowy come?
What compelled him to break from
His prison and make
His way here? What can
He hope to achieve?

SNOWY
(aside)
This is
Getting int'resting.

GEORGE
Would he damage us
More? Would he worsen our state?
Whom have we to blame
But Snowy for our
Banishment? 'Twas his plan or
His ineptitude?

SNOWY
(aside)
I? Inept? The fool!

GEORGE
The rabbit, with his simp'ring
Cloying ways. "Danny,
Let me lead the toys.
Let me be the boss, and I
Will serve you ever."

He's primp'd, prodded, begg'd
His way to power, only
To serve his master
And himself, never
To look after the needs of
The others. Now he
Returns to cement
Our fate. He protects himself.

RECTOR
He obeyed Danny.

GEORGE
That's obedience
To a callow teen. His ought
Was to his fellows.
He has come here to
Whinge and worm his way once more
Into the graces
Of a feckless boy.

He desires to live once more
In comfort and sloth,

Kowtowing to the
Whims of our owner, a child
Who never loved us.

SNOWY
George, that's infamous!

RECTOR
Where did you come from?

SNOWY
To say
He never loved us.

COUNT
I always look 'hind
Every arras. Always
Someone hiding there.

SNOWY and GEORGE
Shut up!

COUNT
Shutting up.
(to RECTOR)
I thought that was an aside.

RECTOR
It was not.

COUNT
Oh, well.

SNOWY
I tried. I begged. What
Could I do?

GEORGE
  You could have fought
For our freedom.

SNOWY
  Fought?

Against what? Against
Aging? We're owed rights, but time
Is not on our side.

GEORGE
Danny could have fought
For us. He could have kept us —
Some of us at least.

He did not weep when
We were banish'd below. He
Shed no tears for us.

He forgot us.

SNOWY
  Oh!
How could he forget? He was
Ever our great friend.

GEORGE
You came hoping for
Reconciliation, but
I came for vengeance.

SNOWY
Danny has a new
Life. I want to be part of
It.

GEORGE
I want our old
Lives back. I will stop
At nothing less. Count's with me.
Are you not, Count?

COUNT
Yes.

SNOWY
Rector, stand by me.

RECTOR
Oh, what should I do?

GEORGE
Stand by
Your master, or live
Free with us.

SNOWY
Come here,
Rector. That's a good boy. It
Is two against two.

As boss, I get to
Break the tie.

GEORGE
  I was first. My
Vote counts for more.

SNOWY
  Say
Not 'first', George. You were
Never the first. Say not 'first'.

GEORGE
True. I was ne'er first.
That madness, that fate,
I avoided. Yet I am
Older. That counts some.

SNOWY
We'll not give you that.

GEORGE
Then we are at an impasse.

RECTOR
What is to be done?

\* \* \* \* \*

# ACT I
## SCENE 3

JOE
(without)
Woman!

BABS
(also without)
Don't 'woman'
Me, you neanderthal. Now,
Get out of my way.

*Enter BABS, a fashion doll, and JOE, an action figure.*

JOE
I found them.

Hi, guys.

BABS
You found them? You're such a jerk.

He wanted breakfast.

JOE
I wanted eggs, but
I could not find them.

BABS
Try the
Refrigerator.

JOE
The door was heavy.

BABS
Boo hoo.

JOE
Careful, Babs. I am
Your lord and master.

BABS
My lord and master.
Ha!

JOE
Spoils of war, you are.

BABS
Watch
It Achilles, or
It won't be your heel
That I kick.

JOE
You hear that, guys?
All I asked for was
A little breakfast.
Was that so much to ask? Guys?

SNOWY
Well....

GEORGE
I don't....

COUNT
P'rhaps....

RECTOR
Uh.

BABS
This is one hell of
A fellowship you've got here,
Snowy.

RECTOR
That is rude.

BABS
Sit. Stay. Good boy.

GEORGE
Look,
Babs. You didn't need to join
Us on this our quest.

BABS
Was I talking to
You, microbrain?

GEORGE
Well.... Uh.... No.

BABS
Then until I do,
Be a good monkey:
No lookee, sayee, hearee.
Kapisch?

GEORGE
Uh…. I…. Yeah.

BABS
So, cottontail. Why
Are we in the TV room?

SNOWY
Is that where we are?

BABS
Did you notice the TV?

SNOWY
Yes…?

BABS
    Not that it is
Much of a TV. Mine took
Up the entire wall.
Satellite. Remote
Control. Video player.
I'd really pimped out
My penthouse.

JOE
    Here we
Go.

BABS
   The perfect place after
A long day at the
Studio or the
Space station. Or better, I
Could take my red sports
Car — Red. Sports. Car. — to
My beach house and lounge on the
Warm sands by the sea.

P'rhaps I'd entertain
Film stars or heads of state in
My gourmet Kitchen.

JOE
She's a cordon bleu
Chef, but she still won't make me
Eggs when I ask her.

BABS
Eggs I have. One of
The few things I was allowed
To take when Rambo
Here kidnapped me.

JOE
   Ha!
Eggs? They're plastic.

BABS
So are you!

COUNT
All this talk of food!

Babs you are looking
Delicious

      BABS
  Are you thinking
What I think you are?

      COUNT
No! Of course I'm not!

      BABS
What happened the last time you
Tried?

      COUNT
  I'm so hungry.

      BABS
Do you remember?

      COUNT
Yes. You punched me in the nose.

      BABS
What did I do then?

      COUNT
Threw me off the bed.

      BABS
And?

COUNT
Dropped a dictionary
On me.

RECTOR
He's in luck.
No dictionaries
Here.

BABS
Did you enjoy that?

COUNT
No.

RECTOR
There's a TV Guide.

BABS
Want that again?

COUNT
No.

RECTOR
No so dangerous, guide for
TV.

BABS
Do you?

COUNT
No.

JOE
Kidnapped!?

GEORGE
Took him long
Enough.

SNOWY
Don't get involved.

JOE
I
Rescued you.

BABS
Rescued?

JOE
You were about to
Be sold in slavery to
A desert sultan.
What depraved things he
Would have done to you.

BABS
And those
Depraved things would be?

JOE
I....don't know. But they
Would have been horrible.

      BABS
  So,
You rescue me from
A palace in an
Oasis, lounging by the
Pool, and being served
By an army of
Eunuchs. And in exchange, I
Get to live in a
Cardboard box.

  At least
The eunuch situation
Hasn't really changed.

      JOE
Babs! You promised you
Wouldn't talk about that.

      BABS
  That's
My lot. Joe, you're a
Real keeper, you are.

My Sally would never have
Abandoned me so.
Had I stayed with her,
I'd still have my homes. My jobs.
I'd be wearing more.

      SNOWY
Then why not leave? Why
Not climb from your box and search
For others. There are

Many voices there,
Among the boxes, among
Our pasts. Certainly,
You could have found one
More to your liking. Perhaps
You'd have found your friends.

BABS
My friends are no more.
When Sally left, her past left
With her.

I heard the
Fights, the anger, things
Said to her family that
Should not have been said.

I wish I had been
With her. Maybe I could have
Comforted her. P'rhaps.

So many times I
Wanted to leave. I did not.
Maybe I could not.

Something held me back.
Don't smirk at me y'egotist.
Not you. I think — I
Guess — I had nowhere
Else to go. No one, none, else.
Had my sisters been
Here, of course, they'd have
Mounted an expedition,
Would have rescued me.

Had some force denied
Them that right, then Kevin would —

> JOE

Kevin?

> BABS

Yes. Kevin.

> JOE

You bring up Kevin?

> BABS

Kevin was a loving and
Loyal man.

> JOE

He wore
Flip flops and pastel
Shirts.

> BABS

That's all you know.

> JOE

That's all
That I need to know.

> BABS

I wish my hair was
Longer.

JOE
Your hair's long enough.


BABS
It doesn't look right.

My sisters and I
Had such long hair. Sally liked
To brush it for us.
Now mine is barely
Long enough e'en to tie back.
It was so pretty.


JOE
Oh, the hair story
Again. Pray she doesn't start
On about her shoes.


BABS
I had so many
Shoes.


JOE
See? What did I say?


SNOWY
You
Did bring up the shoes.


RECTOR
I could eat a shoe.

COUNT
If you ate one of hers, she'd
Punch you in the nose.

JOE
I'll bring up any
Subject I like. I am a
War hero.

BABS
   A war
Hero? Joe cannot
E'en spell the word 'war'.

JOE
   Can too.

BABS
Then how is it spelled?

JOE
With...with...with a gun.
A gun spells both war and peace.

BABS
You know naught of both.

JOE
I know naught?

BABS
   Say I.

JOE
I, who have stormed the very
Gates of Berlin and

Cast down the most vile
Tyranny; I, who have faced
Death. I know of war.

BABS
Hogwash. You could not
Find Germany on a map
If Hitler stood there
Naked and strumming
On a banjo while singing
The Horst Wessel Song.

JOE
Base and cruel woman.
I'm going over there. Don't
Follow me. Do not.

BABS
I'm not following.
I just feel like going there.
I do not know why.

JOE
You always say that.

BABS
Because I always mean that.

JOE
I'm going to sit here.

BABS
And sulk.

JOE
I will brood.
Heroes brood.

BABS
But you will sulk.

JOE
I will brood.

BABS
Kevin
Would contemplate.

JOE
The
Luckiest day of his life?
When I rescued you.

BABS
Brood. Sulk. What have you.

Snowy.

SNOWY
What?

BABS
My question. What
Are we doing here?

SNOWY

I want to return
Home. I want all of us, all,
To be welcomed here.

GEORGE

I've come for vengeance.
We have been imprisoned for
So long. Now is our
Turn. I crave freedom
Just as Snowy, but freedom
At what cost? Do we
Trade one bondage for
Another? The difference
Between box and shelf
Might be little more
Than the view.

SNOWY

That is something.

GEORGE

Something. Yes, something.

This is no longer
A home for children or toys.
Laughter echoes not
In these rooms. Footsteps
Running up and down the stairs
No longer mark time.

Darkness permeates
This place. 'Twere better had we
Not come.

SNOWY
It is night.
The morn will come and
Bring light. Then we will see friend
And foe more clearly.

GEORGE
Yet the darkness will
Prevail. You'll nor find peace here,
Rabbit, nor friendship.

This place once had an
Aroma of joy. Now's naught
But stench of sorrow.

In our prisons we
May have wallowed in pity
And despair. At least,
Though, that was our choice.
Here, at best, we'll be subject
To the whims of a
Master who's shown that
He no longer wants nor needs
Nor even loves us.

SNOWY
Yet, to live up here
And watch life around us. Is
Not that better.

GEORGE
P'rhaps.

P'rhaps hell is to live
So close to paradise, to
Be able to stretch
Out your hands, almost
Able to touch, embrace it,
Knowing you ne'er will.

SNOWY
Perhaps our ends would
Be the same. However, at
Least we would have tried.

GEORGE
So, what would you have
Us do? Should we continue
To look for Danny?

SNOWY
My senses tell me
He is somewhere near.

COUNT
There are
Dark places here, friend.
Places e'en I'd not
Dare.

RECTOR
Should I sneak upstairs?

JOE
No.

Far too dangerous.

RECTOR
Too perilous. Da.

BABS
Typical. I will go there.

JOE
I advise you don't.

BABS
What should I fear there?

SNOWY
The woman in white.

BABS
What is
She to me?

SNOWY
I've seen
Her down in our crypt.
She has no love for dust or
Things from Danny's past.

GEORGE
She's not family.
She would throw us out before
She would keep us.

SNOWY
　　Yet,
I must insist you
Not follow that path. If we
Decide that we must
Then we will make a
Plan.

BABS
　　What plan do you have for
Us now? If we do
Not search, what follows?
Do we return below?

RECTOR
　No.
Say not go below.

GEORGE
Then what?

SNOWY
I don't know.

We sit here. We wait.

GEORGE
We wait.

SNOWY
What would Danny do?

GEORGE
Read a book.

COUNT
Drink some
Blood.

BABS
Really?

COUNT
Have a sandwich?
Please don't hit me.

BABS
Bah!

SNOWY
No. No. Danny would
Have an adventure.

GEORGE
That would
Have been my next guess.

JOE
Have an adventure.
I like it.

COUNT
Me, too.

RECTOR
Let us
Have an adventure.

*They think.*

BABS
Okay, then. Let's go.

*They think.*

SNOWY
What adventure should we have?

GEORGE
Perhaps....

SNOWY
What?

GEORGE
...nothing.

*They think.*

RECTOR
I know! What about
We have adventure on steppes
Of Siberia.

BABS
I am hardly dressed
For Siberia.

JOE
That's all
Right, Babs. Danny once
Said that in Russia,
All women are hot, so you
Should be just fine.

BABS
(To SNOWY)
I
Do not think that is
What Danny meant.

SNOWY
Hush, do not
Confuse him.

RECTOR
Russian
Steppes are wild, wond'rous
Places,

SNOWY
What do we do there?

RECTOR
We chase things.

SNOWY
What things?

RECTOR
(To GEORGE)
Would he be angry
If I said we chase rabbits.

GEORGE
He would.

RECTOR
Nor rabbits.

Nor monkeys.

GEORGE
Good.

JOE
What
About warriors?

RECTOR
Never.

COUNT
Vampires? Not vampires.

RECTOR
Of course nor vampires.

(*To BABS*)
What are you today?

BABS
I am
A neurosurgeon.

SNOWY
A neurosurgeon?

BABS
Yes.

SNOWY
Really?

BABS
Yes. What of it?

SNOWY
Nothing.

RECTOR
Then we don't
Chase neurosurgeons.

GEORGE
What is left?

RECTOR
We chase...skelniks?

BABS
Skelniks?

JOE
Not skelniks!

BABS
What's a skelnik?

GEORGE
'Bout
Four or five pounds.

BABS
(To SNOWY)
What's that mean?

SNOWY
Don't worry. It would
Not be funny, e'en
If it made sense.

RECTOR
Skelniks are
Fierce monsters that live
Beneath the vast plains.
They ride on the winds and hunt
Lonely travellers
And steal their gold. If
We catch them, we get their gold.

COUNT
And three wishes?

RECTOR
Yes.

SNOWY
Then skelniks it is.

*Pause.*

GEORGE
So, what's this skelnik look like?

RECTOR
What?

GEORGE
What's it look like?

RECTOR
Looks like...a...skelnik.

SNOWY
Ah.

BABS
Then where is it?

RECTOR
It is....
Perhaps it's back there.

GEORGE
Back there?

RECTOR
P'rhaps it is.

SNOWY
Why not go.

RECTOR
It's very dark.

JOE
I've no night goggles.

BABS
Any of you? You're so brave.

JOE
Why don't you go, Babs?

*Pause.*

BABS
I'm...not...dressed...for...dark.

SNOWY
Well then, George?

GEORGE
An adventure
In the jungle.

SNOWY
Great!

So, what do we do?

GEORGE
We climb a tree.

*They look around.*

SNOWY
Is that one?

GEORGE
Could be.

SNOWY
Let's go then.

*They all climb.*

BABS
And?

GEORGE
We look around.

RECTOR
What are we looking for?

GEORGE
Some
Mysterious thing.

SNOWY
What is it?

GEORGE
I don't
Know.

RECTOR
P'rhaps that's the mystery.

GEORGE
I see it! O'er there!

BABS
That's…! That's...a...remote.

RECTOR
Nothing mysterious 'bout
A TV remote.

GEORGE
Sorry, guys.

COUNT
We could
Sack a village.

SNOWY
That sounds good.

COUNT
Then drain the blood of
Maidens we find there.

SNOWY
Ew!

COUNT
And grow strong, powerful.

BABS
Drain their blood?

COUNT
Tasty!

BABS
Could I have sushi instead?

COUNT
Sushi? What's the point?

Plenty of maidens
To go around. Why else would
You sack a village?

JOE
I know! I know! We
Could storm an enemy beach. Dodge
Bullets, explosions.
Fight up the shingle,
Establish a beachhead, and
We could be gunned down,
Dying in a blaze
Of glory.

BABS
We'd be dead!

JOE
We
Would all die heroes.

BABS
I'm not inviting
You to my beach house if Joe
Wants to invade it.

Would anyone like
To attend a board meeting
At my company?

GEORGE
Is that what you do
For fun?

SNOWY
Be nice.

GEORGE
I'm being
Nice.

BABS
Absolutely.

No takers? Your loss.

SNOWY
We could bounce.

GEORGE
Bounce?

SNOWY
Bounce.

GEORGE
Why would
We want to do that?

SNOWY
Because it's great fun.

GEORGE
We've got nothing else to lose.

SNOWY
Try it. Let's all bounce.

*They hop.*

Higher. Higher! Great!

*They hop higher.*

RECTOR
Sorry, but that's not much fun.

BABS
Are we bouncing right?

SNOWY
It has been a while
Since I last bounced. Maybe we
Are doing it wrong.

JOE
No, the technique is
Simple enough. Fast. Slow. Hard.
Soft. It seems...not fun.

SNOWY
It's….It's...what we do.

GEORGE
Really? You bounce? You just bounce?

SNOWY
Isn't 'just' bouncing.
It's what rabbits do.

GEORGE
Why do it then?

SNOWY
It's bouncing.

GEORGE
It seems so pointless.

SNOWY
No more pointless than
Climbing trees.

GEORGE
Say you?

SNOWY
Say I.

BABS
I've an idea.

I think...I think we
Should cast off our burdens and
Relax upon the sands
That stretch along
A playful sea, and enjoy
The sun's soothing rays.

JOE
What?

BABS
I said that we
Should cast off our burdens and
Relax on the sands
That stretch along
A playful sea, and enjoy
The sun's soothing rays.

JOE
You want to sit...sit!...
On the sand.

BABS
Nay 'sit'. Recline.

JOE
Can we storm the beach?

BABS
You can't 'storm the beach'.
You can recline on the sand.

JOE
Why would I do that?

BABS
Because it is fun.

JOE
It is dangerous.

BABS
How so?

JOE
You might get shot.

BABS
Shot?

JOE
When we storm the beach.

RECTOR
You could get run over by
A tank.

JOE
Yes! A tank!

BABS
No tanks on my beach.

JOE
When I storm a beach, I have
Tanks.

RECTOR
Artillery?

JOE
Yes! Artillery!

SNOWY
Don't encourage him, Rector.

BABS
You ne'er stormed a beach.

JOE
I did too. We were
In the backyard. I was most
Heroic.

BABS
Sure, Joe.

JOE
Really heroic.
Back me up, guys. Guys? I was
Really...really...brave.

SNOWY
Having fun use to
Be much easier.

GEORGE
Were I
Boss, I —

SNOWY
What, George? What
Would you have done?
Would you have kept us from the
Boxes.

GEORGE
I'd have tried.

SNOWY
How?

GEORGE
I...do not...know.


SNOWY
Then keep your mouth shut. We need
Ideas, not gripes.

Did you lead us here?
I listened to you complain
For years, yet you ne'er
Even suggested
We try to come up here. Why
Not? But when I do,
And you have straggled
Along at the rear of our
Procession, then you
Know what I did wrong.


GEORGE
I do not like it here.


SNOWY
    I
Don't like it either.

I know not this place.
Yes, it may be our house, but
It is not our home.
Naught but a ling'ring
Whiff of the familiar.
There's no light. No life.
The furniture is
Wrong. I recognize nothing.

Where are the other
Toys? The games? Laughter?
Music? Here's antiseptic.

GEORGE
You promised that you'd
Find us Danny. Where
Is he?

SNOWY
I do not know, George.

GEORGE
Until he is here
To blame, I will say
That you are responsible.

SNOWY
I'm responsible?

GEORGE
You are the boss, no?

BABS
Guys.

SNOWY
Back off, banana breath.

BABS
Guys.

GEORGE
Make me big ears.
I'll tie them around —

*They fight.*

SNOWY
You let go of me. Rector!

*RECTOR joins in.*

GEORGE
Ouch!

COUNT
And no one punched
You in the nose.

SNOWY
Back
Off, dead man.

COUNT
You take that back.

*COUNT joins in the fray.*

RECTOR
Howl!

GEORGE
Gotcha, Rover.

COUNT
You cannot hit me!
You cannot hit me!

SNOWY
Stand still,
Will you!

BABS
You're going

To make too much noise.
We will get in —

> *The fighters tumble into BABS.*

Hey!

JOE
When Babs
Says, "be still," Be still!

> *Everyone freezes.*
> *GEORGE is holding a cushion.*

BABS
Put that down.

GEORGE
Make me.

SNOWY
George, do not be a fool.

> *With a roar, GEORGE throws the cushion.*

ALL (save GEORGE)

No!

*The cushion flies into the shadowy area of the room.*
*There is a crash.*

SNOWY

Oh.

DANNY
(In the shadows)
What? Who? Who's there?

RECTOR

I'm scared, Snowy.

SNOWY

Hush.

GEORGE

Oh, crap.

DANNY

I said, 'who's there?'

*DANNY turns on his lamp.*
*He is revealed, lying in his bed.*
*DANNY is a very old and frail-looking man.*

*He and the others spend a long moment looking at each other.*

ALL

Ah!

— End of Act I —

* * * * *

# ACT II
## SCENE 1

*Immediately following.*
*There need not be a break.*

DANNY
Who...who...who…

GEORGE
We've found
And owl. An old one, by the
Look of him.

SNOWY
Hush, George.
He is an old man.

DANNY
Who are you?

GEORGE
Your worst nightmare.

DANNY
Help, ho! Help, ho! Nurse!

GEORGE
Shut him up, Rector.

SNOWY
Leave him alone.

GEORGE
Bite him! You're
A Russian Wolfhound.

COUNT
We will tie him up.

SNOWY
You'll do nothing of the sort.
He has not harmed us.

GEORGE
He will call for the
Woman in white, and then we
Will be sent below.

DANNY
Nurse! Will not someone
Come?

SNOWY
Quiet, sir. We will not
Harm you. But quiet.

COUNT
I could drink his blood.
Strengthened, I could then face the
Woman in white. Yes.

SNOWY
No. Babs?

BABS
He means naught
To me. Your...our quest has failed.
Let's return below.

DANNY
Return below or
Go out. I will call again.
At some point, she'll hear.

GEORGE
It took all our will
To make the great trek here. I
Would not go back yet.

DANNY
Then leave me. Be you
Dream be you nightmare, leave me
To mine own terrors.

GEORGE
This old man has spied
On us. Do not let him then
Banish us.

JOE
Kill him!

DANNY
Oh! Oh!

SNOWY
That's enough!

You have nothing to fear from
Us. We're on a quest
To escape from our
Prison and enjoy this place.
You are free to go.

DANNY
I cannot leave.

GEORGE
    We
Can compel you.

DANNY
    You've escaped
Your prison. Mine's here.
This bed's my prison,
My fate. I've not left in months.

I fear I will not
Leave it again.

SNOWY
    Then
We will leave you. We'll find whom
We are looking for
In another room.

DANNY
There's none but me and the nurse.
There are no others.

It is an empty
Place. If you go forth then you
Will surely be caught.

GEORGE
Now he wants us to
Stay.

Would you call again for
The woman in white?

DANNY
She rarely comes here.
When she does, she looks and sees
Signs of life then leaves.

GEORGE
Don't we terrify
You?

DANNY
Far less terrifying
Than being alone.

GEORGE
We shan't entertain
You, old man. We have a quest.
We seek our master.

DANNY
There are no masters
Here. Only a slave to death
Awaiting his call.

GEORGE
Come along, Snowy.

SNOWY
We will leave you, sir.

Danny
Must be otherwhere.

*They start to leave.*

DANNY
Danny. Danny. Oh.
So long since I've heard that name.
So many years since.

SNOWY
Then, he's no longer
Here.

I'm sorry, guys. Perhaps
It is best we go.

*They continue to leave.*

DANNY
Rector?

RECTOR
Huh?

DANNY
Rector.
They called you 'Rector'.

RECTOR
I am
Rector.

DANNY
You are he!

And you...are...Snowy?

SNOWY
Yes, I am. What of it?

GEORGE
We
Should be going, guys.

DANNY
Do not go. Rector,
Come here. Do you not know me?
Can you not smell me?

*RECTOR does.*

RECTOR
You're...you're...Danny!

DANNY
That was the name of my youth,
So so long ago.

RECTOR
You're Danny!

Snowy,
Is Danny!

SNOWY
I don't think so,
Rector. He's so old.

DANNY
Yes. Old. Yet I do
Remember the friends I played
With so long ago.

RECTOR
Danny! We missed you!

SNOWY
If you are indeed he, we
Came to look for you.

DANNY
And found me you have.
Where have you been, my friends?

Count?
Still looking for blood?

COUNT
It must be Danny.

GEORGE
Must it?

DANNY
Still angry, George?

GEORGE
Grmph!

DANNY
Certainly surly.

SNOWY
He's got you there, George.

GEORGE
I have my doubts.

RECTOR
I've got it.
What is a Skelnik?

DANNY
(*Thinks*)
'Bout four or five pounds.

*The two laugh.*

SNOWY
It still isn't funny.

DANNY
Don't
Be so literal.

And my warrior.

JOE
Hoo-rah!

DANNY
Hoo-rah!

*He has a short coughing fit.*

Yes. Indeed.

BABS
No kind words for Babs?

DANNY
You...are one of my
Sister's...one of Sally's toys.

JOE
Don't you remember?
We rescued —

BABS
Kidnapped.

JOE
— Her.

DANNY
Yes.  A great adventure.

BABS
Not for the victim.

DANNY
You had no great life.

BABS
I lived in splendor, lux'ry.
My sisters and I
Ruled our world as well as men,
But with style, glamour.
Sally loved me.

DANNY
She —

BABS
Loved us. She treated us like
We were princesses.

He kidnapped...you stole
Me.

Let them love you if they
Will. I'll none of it.
You cared not for my
Hopes, my tears. You cared not for
Sally's. I will go.

DANNY
Then go.

BABS
I will.

JOE
Go,
If you like, though I will stay.
I've had it with you.

BABS
My feet point at the
Door, but I can't bring myself
To go on through it.

Why is that, old man?

JOE
No one is stopping you. Go!
The door is there, Babs.

BABS
Why cannot I go?
Just as you robbed me of her,
You've robbed me of will.

Sally loved me. What
Tears she must have wept when I
Was taken from her.

DANNY
None.

BABS
None? Nonsense. I
Was her favorite.

DANNY
She knew

Not you were taken.

### BABS
How could she not know?

My sisters would have cried for
Me. They'd have told her.
We were a team, my
Sisters and I. Equally
Cherished and adored.

### DANNY
She bobbed your locks, and
When your hair would not grow back
Threw you in a box.

### BABS
No! That is not true.

### DANNY
You lingered there, alone, for
Years 'til Joe found you.

### BABS
You lie.

### JOE
   I recall
It well, Babs. We took you home.
Your sisters, in their
Finery, once yours,
Laughed at you, rejected you.
You were imperfect.
So, they cast you out.

Where else could you go but with
Us?

We rescued you.

We clothed you.

BABS
You call
This clothing?

DANNY
A handkerchief
Was all that I had.

BABS
Men. No, not men — boys.

DANNY
I thought it looked cute.

BABS
I don't.

DANNY
Then do not wear it.

*The others chuckle.*
*DANNY starts coughing.*

SNOWY
Are you all right?

DANNY
It
Will pass. Give me some water.

RECTOR
Get him some water!

SNOWY
Water! Water!

GEORGE
If
He is indeed Danny, he
Is no use to us.

SNOWY
Give him water, I
Say.

> *SNOWY and GEORGE glare at each other.*

GEORGE
(finally)
Count. Give him water.

DANNY
There
On the table.

> *COUNT gives him water.*
> *DANNY drinks. His coughing subsides.*

Thanks.

GEORGE
This man cannot play.
He's of no use to us, be
He Danny or no.

DANNY
I am old. I'm no
Longer made for sports and games.

GEORGE
You were still young when
You sent us away.

DANNY
Yes. I was.

GEORGE
You did not love
Us.

DANNY
I did love you.

SNOWY
Then why did you send
Us away?

DANNY
You are children's
Toys, and I grew up.

GEORGE
That is no excuse.

DANNY
P'rhaps. But it is a reason.

GEORGE
It's not good enough.

DANNY
What reason would be?
What do you want me to say?
That I ne'er loved you?

You were my life, my
Childhood. I recall the games,
The grand adventures.

GEORGE
A childhood and the
Adventures you have forgot.

DANNY
No! Say not forgot!

SNOWY
We did not forget.

GEORGE
Why did you forsake us?

DANNY
   Why?
Because I grew up.

GEORGE
And in the growing,
Was there not a place for us?
Had we no purpose?

DANNY
You served your purpose.
When I was a child and was
Confined to this place,
You had a purpose.
When my journeys took me out
To venture beyond
These walls, that fence, how
Could you have joined me there?

GEORGE
    We
Could have tried. We would

Never have left you.

DANNY
I went to school, got a job,
Had a wife...children.

GEORGE
Whom we would have loved
As much as we had loved you.
You abandoned us.

DANNY
They had toys of their
Own. They would not have wanted
My dusty relics.

GEORGE

You owe us.

DANNY

   Owe you?
I gave you life...voice. I gave
You your adventures.

You were masters as
Much as I. When I grew, when
I left, I had to
Throw off my youth, my
Past, for life must move forward.
My future needed
All my love, my thoughts.

GEORGE

Did it need your memories,
Those we cannot share?

DANNY

Your memories are
Better than mine. You are but
Distant dreams from a
Time — I'll not call it
Happier, for I loved my
Wife, loved my children —
I'll say easier.

GEORGE

What then becomes of us?

DANNY
   You
Have your memories.
There is joy in that.
I'm glad that you remember
Those glorious days,
For there are none left
Who do. My parents, sister,
They are all gone now.
My wife is gone as
Well, as are her memories
Of our adventures.
My children indulged
Me. They had their own hopes, dreams,
Their own fantasies.
My grandchildren? Well,
They love me, but I am but
An obligation.
As for their children —
I will be little more than
A hazy mem'ry
At best. Perhaps they
Will know my name. There will be
Photographs, but there'll
Not be adventures
To recall. Not of mine. No.
Not too long from now,
You will preserve the
Last of my memories. For
That, I am grateful.

GEORGE

So, my last mem'ry
Of you will e'er be of when
I was cast away.

SNOWY

Let it go, George.

GEORGE

  Ne'er
Will I. You were not there. You
Do not remember.

DANNY

I was fourteen, George.
What should a boy at that age
Do when his friends mock
Him and knock him to
The ground and laugh and jeer at
His childish playthings?

At some point I had
To grow up. I had to play
Ball and to meet girls.

GEORGE

You abandoned us.
So, we will abandon you.
I'll make new mem'ries.

SNOWY

How will you do that?

GEORGE
I know I'm not wanted here.
Count, you are with me.

*The toys begin to leave.*
*SNOWY waits.*

DANNY
Go, Snowy. Go. I
Put you in charge for a good
Reason. Care for them.

SNOWY
I hoped to find you
Again.

DANNY
    And found me you have.
I am an old man.
The Danny you sought
Is long gone. Have good mem'ries
Of him. Please go now.

*SNOWY starts to go.*
*RECTOR stops.*

\* \* \* \* \*

# ACT II
## SCENE 2


RECTOR
What is a Skelnik?

DANNY
What's that?

RECTOR
What is a Skelnik?

SNOWY
Rector, come along.

DANNY
A Skelnik? Ah, yes.
The Skelnik. A fearsome beast.
He haunts the vast steppes
Of Siberia.
Older than the howling winds,
More terrifying
Than the freezing nights.
It is his voice that you hear
'Cross the frozen plains.

RECTOR
Can it send a chill
E'en into the stoutest hearts?

DANNY
It can.

RECTOR
So I've heard.

SNOWY
It is time to go.

RECTOR
Wait. Danny, could...could I...could
I face the Skelnik?

*GEORGE reenters.*

GEORGE
We should go.

RECTOR
Could I?

DANNY
I don't know, Rector. It's long
Since I have seen one.

The dreaded Skelnik
Has hidden himself deep in
Vast mountain caverns.
He is safe therein.
Wherefore would he brave our bright
World? He is content.

RECTOR
Can we draw him out?

*The others are in by now.*

DANNY
We need something to tempt him.

BABS
I know where this goes.

DANNY
A lonely girl, lost
In the blowing snows.

BABS
   In the
Snow? I've a parka —
At least I used to
Have a parka…. Had fur coats.

RECTOR
Do you have them now?

BABS
No.

RECTOR
   Then all the more
Peril for you to be in.

DANNY
Wand'ring. Lost. Forlorn.

BABS
Fleeing from a mad
And lustful boyar intent
On stealing my youth...
My innocence.

ALL (save BABS)
Babs!

BABS
What?
Why else would I wander in
The snows half naked?

RECTOR
She's ruining it!

DANNY
Lost from a rich caravan,
Her absence unseen.

BABS
Her hair shorn by the
Jealous wife of the Wagon
Master.

RECTOR
Danny!

DANNY
Babs!

JOE
I'd like to see where
This goes.

BABS
Oh, very well.

DANNY
Lost.
Alone. The blizzard
Snows pelt her. They blind
Her. Where is her family?
Where...where are her friends?

BABS
Where is my fam'ly?
Where are my friends? Joe? Joe? Where
Are you?

JOE
I'm here, Babs!
I'll save you!

DANNY
He's not
Here. He can't save you.

JOE
I'm not
Here. I can't save you.

BABS
Joe is not here. He
Can't save me! What shall I do?

GEORGE
Beware the Skelnik.

It bursts from the snow!

DANNY
It creeps from its hidden lair.

GEORGE
It creeps from its lair.

SNOWY
It pulls itself out,
The many-headed Skelnik,

COUNT
And spies the lost lass.

BABS
Lost, nearly naked.
Her voluptuous body —

GEORGE
Danny!

DANNY
Babs!

BABS
All right!

JOE
The many-headed
Skelnik. Our jaws

SNOWY
Smack

COUNT
And gnaw.

We spy the forlorn
Girl and pounce.

BABS
(*Bored*)
Please help.

RECTOR
Danny! She isn't —

BABS
What? I
Said the words.

RECTOR
Mean them!

BABS
I do not feel them.
I'm master of krav magaw.
Or am I mistress?

SNOWY
You're gonna be food
For the famished Skelnik.

DANNY
Babs?

BABS
Oh, very well. HELP!!!

RECTOR
That I believe. Babs!
I'm coming! Damn you, Skelnik!
Unhand that woman.

SNOWY
I'm hungry! I eat
Woman first.

COUNT
Then eat puppy.

RECTOR
Not puppy, but hound.

Leave off the maiden
So I can thrash you, Skelnik.
I will pounce.

JOE
I'll dodge.

RECTOR
I'll fight the dreaded
Beast.

SNOWY
I'll defend my homeland
And fend for my food.

*RECTOR fights the Skelnik.*

DANNY
Epically, they
Struggle 'gainst one another.

BABS
I've ne'er seen the like.

DANNY
In the end, though, the
Skelnik prevails.

RECTOR
I lose?

DANNY
Yep.

SNOWY
That means we eat!

COUNT, GEORGE, and JOE
(*Greatly rejoicing*)
Yay!

RECTOR
How can Rector lose?

I die, friends. Gather to hear
My words.

DANNY
You're not dead.

RECTOR
How can I not be
Slain, for Rector would not yield
To this base Skelnik.

Say that I breathe my
Last as my blood stains the snow.
But from that blood will
Spring forth great monsters
That will hunt down the Skelnik
And avenge my death.

Oh, friends, hear final
Cries of this ferocious hound
Ere his spirit fails.

DANNY
He dies.
BABS
Great Rector
Failed me.

Oh, I am lost, I.
Lost and alone in
This Siberian waste.
Who will hear these, my cries, now?
Who'll come to save Babs?

SNOWY
The dread Skelnik roars,
Abandons the beaten hound,
And turns to his prey.

DANNY
Yet, her cries did not
Go unheard.

    Far away, in
His tow'r, the Count hears.

COUNT
There, using magicks
Long forbidden, long forgot
'Neath God's jealous gaze,
The Count, lord of the
Mountains and valleys, reaches
Out his dark fingers
And smites down the dread
Skelnik.

SNOWY
    Alas. Our fell corpse
Falls next to Rector's.

BABS
And I am lifted,
Carried upon the winds to
The Count's dark dungeons.

COUNT
There to await my
Pleasure...my will. Though I am
Fearsome, my lady,
The terror that 'waits
You when I feed will also
Bring you great power,
For though the Skelnik

Feeds, it must, must, kill. He brings
Naught but destruction.
I, lady, create.
I drink, I take, but then I
Give eternal life.

Will you join with me?
Take your place by my side to
Rule over these lands.

### BABS
At last, an offer
Worthy of me. Power! And
Wealth?

### COUNT
Great wealth.

### BABS
Goody!

I will accept your
Embrace, my Count.

### JOE
Danny!

### DANNY
Wait.
That's not how it ends.

### BABS
Why not? Allow me
Power. I shall be the dark,

Terrible lady.
I have e'er been the
Damsel. Let me but this once
Achieve position.

JOE
She's not playing fair.
Let me stop her, Danny. I
Will charge in and —

DANNY
No!

COUNT
I approach the cell
Where the sleeping damsel lies.

BABS
Sleeping?

COUNT
Sleeping.

BABS
No.
I will face my fate,
My apotheosis, with
Open willing arms.

JOE
Danny!

COUNT
I pull the
Great door slowly open. There
I spy my victim.
Her slight body lies
Draped across a bed of straw.
Her breast heaves gently.
Her breath leaves a slight
Mist as it passes through her
Soft lips. Her bare throat
Perfect, blemishless,
Inviting me, longing for
The prick of my fangs.

*Long pause.*

BABS
Well?

COUNT
Well?

BABS
Do it, then.

COUNT
Uh….

JOE
Danny! This is wrong.

DANNY
Well….

BABS
What are you going
To do?

COUNT
Well....

BABS
My breasts heave! Lips,
Soft. Neck, inviting.

Do something!

COUNT
Well, I...
Never got this far before.
Not sure what to do.

BABS
You don't know?!

COUNT
Sorry.

BABS
Typical man.

SNOWY
What a let
Down.

COUNT
Danny. Help me.

JOE
I'd know what to do.

BABS
You're such a neanderthal.

JOE
And him?

BABS
He's a Count.

COUNT
Yes. I am a Count.
I...I...I come slowly in.
I approach the lass.

GEORGE
Who's no longer there!

COUNT
Where is she?

GEORGE
I heard her cries
And came and took her.

JOE
Thought she was asleep.

BABS
You haven't thought in years.

JOE
Hey!
That's not nice.

BABS
Shut up.

GEORGE
On my vine, I swing
From my jungle lair.

I take
The lass.

We're away.

BABS
I fight.

GEORGE
You're asleep.

BABS
I want to be a countess.

GEORGE
I don't care.

BABS
Danny!

DANNY
The mighty monkey
Swoops in and carries off the
Damsel.

COUNT
I give chase.

GEORGE
I swing through the trees,
Across valleys, up mountains.

COUNT
And the Count gives chase.

GEORGE
None swings faster by
Vine than George!

COUNT
I fly using
Magic.

BABS
Help! Oh, help!

JOE
Quiet, woman! It's
A chase scene.

SNOWY
This I gotta
Watch.

RECTOR
What's up?

SNOWY
Sh!

JOE
Watch!

> SNOWY, RECTOR, JOE, and DANNY watch the chase.

Watch out!

BABS
Oh! Woah!

RECTOR
Duck!

DANNY
Oh, my!

JOE
That's gotta hurt! Babs!

COUNT
Oh, ha!

JOE
I can't watch!

GEORGE
It's no good. I can't
Maneuver!

RECTOR
Stay on target.

GEORGE
He's too close!

RECTOR
Stay on

Target.

GEORGE
Loosen up!

DANNY
He bursts through the trees.

COUNT
Followed
Closely by the Count.

GEORGE
Only to come face-
To-face with the Sun!

COUNT
The Sun!
My great enemy
And bane to my kind.
Oh! Dear friends —

DANNY
He dies.

COUNT
I die?

DANNY
Yes.

COUNT
No.

DANNY
Yes.

COUNT
But what
Of my monologue?

SNOWY
More of a soliloquy.

COUNT
But you would be here.

SNOWY
Yet not listening.

COUNT
Not fair. Why can I not speak
When Rector got to?

SNOWY
If they monologue
Like that, I'll go home during
The intermission.

RECTOR

Only four stanzas.

COUNT

Still....

DANNY

You burst into flames. The
Ash drifts to the ground.

GEORGE

So, I have captured
Babs.

BABS

What will you do, you beast?
You can not have me.

GEORGE

I will carry Babs
To a narrow strip of sand,
Bound on one side by
A lush jungle filled
With an infinite number
Of dangerous beasts,
On the other by
A roaring pounding surf that
Beats rock to powder.

DANNY

Huh?

GEORGE

What?

DANNY
  I did not
Follow what you said.

JOE
  Kinda
Confusing, George.

GEORGE
  Oh.

I will carry Babs
To a narrow strip of sand,
Bound on one side by
A lush jungle filled
With an infinite number
Of dangerous beasts,
On the other by
A roaring pounding surf that
Beats rock to powder.

RECTOR
Hmm.

DANNY
  Still a little
Unclear.

GEORGE
  I'm taking her to
The beach.

DANNY
  I get it.

BABS
The beach? In these clothes?
Couldn't I wear a bathing
Suit and also heels?

RECTOR
You'd plenty of time
To change.

BABS
In the dungeon or
Swinging on the vine?

JOE
A minute ago
Poor Babs was half naked. Now
She is overdressed.

GEORGE
You are a captive.
I am tying you to the
Banana tree here.

SNOWY
(aside)
Bananas do not
Grow on trees.

DANNY
Don't talk to the
Audience.

SNOWY
Sorry.

GEORGE
I'm tying you to
The tree.

SNOWY
The plant.

GEORGE
I'm tying
You to this here lamp.

BABS
But I will be hot.

GEORGE
Wear whatever you damn well
Please.

BABS
Is this better?

*BABS is now, somehow, wearing a bathing suit and heels.*

GEORGE
I'm not sure.

DANNY
It is…
Quite all right, Babs.

SNOWY
You're a lot
Diff'rent than you were.

DANNY
Age does that, Snowy.
I just ne'er saw Babs...as...as...
So...so....

ALL (save DANNY)
What!?

DANNY
...Go on.

GEORGE
Let the drums sound. Call
Forth birds to sing songs to our
Ancient gods. Cry out
To the skies. Send forth
My challenge. Come all who would
Steal from me my prize.
This is my kingdom.
Despair, for I am mighty
And will vanquish you.

BABS
Oh-do-come-save-me-
Really-anyone-save-me.

JOE
Way to sell it, Babs.

BABS
Fine. Oh! Help! Save me
From this fearsome chimp.

GEORGE
Chimp!?

BABS
From
This terrible ape!

GEORGE
Don't oversell it.

Who will challenge me? Who will
Face this fearsome beast?

SNOWY
I just want to bounce.

RECTOR
I'm dead.

COUNT
Disintegrated.

DANNY
I'm too old.

JOE
All right!

I will fight for you.

GEORGE
You cannot win on my beach.

JOE
I can...in my tank!

GEORGE
Where'd you get a tank?

JOE
Behind this dune.

GEORGE
Not fair!

JOE
Is!

GEORGE
Danny!

DANNY
It's...a...tank.

GEORGE
Well, then. I have a
Tank, too.

JOE
How original.

GEORGE
And mine is bigger!

JOE
Danny!

DANNY
The size of
The tank does not matter.

BABS
If
I had a nickel.

*The 'tanks maneuver'. They 'fire' 'shells' at each other.*

GEORGE
Ha, ha! You missed!

JOE
Dag
Nabbit!

BABS
Ouch! Don't shoot at me
You moron!

JOE
Sorry.

SNOWY
(*Aside*)
Imagine all that
We could do if we had a
Much bigger budget.

DANNY
Stop talking to the
Audience.

GEORGE
Woosh!

BABS
Watch out, Joe!

GEORGE
I got you!

JOE
Oh, no!

GEORGE
I win!

JOE
Not yet, chimp.
Just before I jump from my
Burning tank, I fire.

DANNY
A hit!

GEORGE
Ah! I die!
Remember, enemies and
Friends, that I was brave,
That I defended
My homeland and captive with
Courage and honor.
Care for my subjects,
Conquerer —

JOE

I fire again!

GEORGE

Ouch!

DANNY

It is finished.

JOE

I come, fair lady.
I come for you. I have braved
The mountainous swells
Of an angry sea,
The deadly thundering surf.
Who else would dare?

Thy cry for help was
Heard by all heroes, cowards,
Through the many lands.
Yet, only I came.
Why? Because only I adore,
Only I love you.

Let me love you, dear'st.
Let me take you in my arms.
Let me embrace you.
Let our breaths mingle.
Heart to heart, let the rhythm
Of the beats transform
Us from two to one.
Eyes, the envy of the stars
Flick'ring b'yond the skies,
Turn your gaze to mine

And let my soul be warmed by
Yours.

Let the seas dry,
The sands blow way.
Let mountains fall, then let them
Thrust into the skies
Once more, twice, nay, a
Thousand times.

I care not for
The fates of man nor
Beast nor even the
Briefness of the lives of Gods.
One moment an age,
One age a moment.
Time stops when I am with you.
Let our eyes hold gaze.

Let our lips embrace.
Let our fingers entwine, palm
To palm, flesh to flesh.

Let heaven and its
Angels envy our love, for
They will ne'er have it.

All food, all air, all
Warmth, all hope, all happiness
Comes t'me from your arms.

Know I love only
You, ever you. Lift my soul
By loving me back.

Personne ne comprend point
Pourquoi je vous adore.
Mais, je me rêve des embrasses comme
Des vents tranquilles.

Personne ne comprend point
Pourquoi j'ai besoin de vous.
Mais, vous êtes l'air qui est
Mon haleine.

Personne ne comprend point
Pourquoi Je vous aime.
Mais
Sans vous il n'y a point de rêves
Sans vous il n'y a point d'embrasses
Sans vous il n'y a point d'air
Sans vous il n'y a point de l'haleine
Sans vous il n'y a point de point.

*Pause.*

BABS
Wow!

JOE
I've given you
Poetry, and your reply
Is naught else but 'Wow!'?

BABS
I don't oft say 'Wow!',
So when I do, I like to
Think it means something.

Pretty words you give,
So I must reply in kind:
Take me in your arms.

*They kiss...for an uncomfortably long time.*

SNOWY
(Aside to DANNY)
French?

DANNY
I minored in
French in college.

SNOWY
I did not
Know that.

DANNY
You weren't there.

BABS and JOE
Wow!

*They kiss again.*

GEORGE
Ew!

RECTOR
Stop that!

COUNT
Yuck!

SNOWY
Danny!

DANNY
I...uh…. Oh, sorry.
Snowy, it's your turn.

SNOWY
Behold! My spaceship!

JOE
Ooh! A spaceship! Cool!

BABS
Hey!

RECTOR
That's
Nice.

COUNT
Sleak.

BABS
Guys.

JOE
Will it

Hold us all?

BABS
Guys.

                SNOWY
        Sure.
Hop on in.

                BABS
        Guys.

                JOE
        Move over.

                RECTOR
Can I steer it?

                SNOWY
        No.

It is my spaceship.

                GEORGE
Really cool.

                SNOWY
        Thanks.

                GEORGE
Let's go!

                BABS
Guys!!!

Someone untie me.

JOE (*untying BABS*)
Sorry. You should have
Said something. Ouch! C'mon. Get in.

BABS
You're an idiot.

DANNY
Where are we going?

SNOWY
The Planet of the Bunnies!

JOE (*lecherously*)
Bunnies! Ouch! Sorry.

RECTOR
How fast will it go?

SNOWY
Really fast.

RECTOR
How fast?

SNOWY
Really,
Really fast.

RECTOR
That fast?

ALL (*save SNOWY*)
Cool!

SNOWY
Let's go! Hold on!
Woosh!

COUNT
Watch out for that star!

RECTOR
Ouch!
You burnt my tail.

SNOWY
Oops.

I will slipstream that
Comet.

GEORGE
Whoo hoo!

BABS
I'm falling.

JOE
I have got you, Babs.

I'll always have you.

BABS
Oh, Joe. You're so manly.

*They start kissing again.*

SNOWY
　There
Goes our 'G' rating.

DANNY
The spaceship streaks 'cross
The skies, searching for the small
Distant green planet.

There it is! And we
Approach cautiously. So not
To scare anyone.

Finally, Snowy
Finds his spot and lands his ship.
We all disembark.

SNOWY
Nor mountains. Nor seas
To flood, nor storms to frighten.
Naught but rolling glade.

BABS
It's so beautiful.

COUNT
Is it where bunnies come to
Die?

SNOWY
　No. It is where

Bunnies come...to bounce!

RECTOR
To bounce?

SNOWY
Yes. Try it.

COUNT
Not I.

SNOWY
Give it a try.

C'mon!

Start with a simple
Hop. Not bad, Danny. Good job,
Babs. Now, hop again.

COUNT
That's more of a jump.

GEORGE
I'm hopping fine.

COUNT
You're skipping.

SNOWY
Skipping is fine, too.

Now, guys, try a bounce.
Bend your knees then leap. Throw your
Ears up to the sky.

BABS
His ears are bigger
Than yours.

JOE
That is not my fault.

BABS
They are still bigger.

SNOWY
Bounce!

COUNT (*hesitantly*)
Bounce.

RECTOR
Bounce.

DANNY (*carefully*)
Bounce.

BABS
Bounce.

*They are momentarily distracted, watching BABS bounce.*
*SNOWY nudges GEORGE.*

GEORGE
Bounce.

JOE
Bounce. Oops.

SNOWY
Doing fine, Joe!
Now. All together.


ALL
Bounce, bounce, bounce, bounce, bounce.
Bounce, bounce, bounce, bounce, bounce, bounce, bounce.
Bounce, bounce, bounce, bounce, bounce.

Bounce, bounce, bounce, bounce, bounce.
Bounce, bounce, bounce, bounce, bounce, bounce, bounce.
Bounce, bounce, bounce, bounce, bounce.

Bounce, bounce, bounce, bounce, bounce.
Bounce, bounce, bounce, bounce, bounce, bounce, bounce.
Bounce, bounce, bounce, bounce, bounce.

*That is, they bounce for a while.*

*They all collapse, laughing and exhausted.*

\* \* \* \* \*

# ACT II
## SCENE 3

SNOWY
That was wonderful.
Let's do it again.

DANNY
Maybe
Later. I'm worn out.

JOE
It's been a while since
I've bounced so.

BABS
It's been a while
Since you bounced so long!

JOE
Not cool!

BABS
Lighten up.

RECTOR
Did I miss something?

DANNY
I don't
Think you want to know.

COUNT
I want another
Story.

BABS
Yes, Danny.

DANNY
I'm tired.

RECTOR
One more adventure.

DANNY
No. Maybe later.

JOE
Come on!

GEORGE
Please! I'll fly a blimp
This time.

COUNT
Please, Danny!

SNOWY
But soft! Someone comes.
There is a noise without.

BABS
Oh!

*Indeed, there is a noise without.*
*Someone, or something, approaches.*

GEORGE
What shall we do?

JOE
Fight!

RECTOR
Hide. Let's hide, Danny.

BABS
It's too close!

COUNT
What shall we do?

SNOWY
It's here!

*The door opens.*
*BEAR enters. BEAR is old and worn from too much love.*

ALL (*save BEAR*)
Ah!

BEAR
Danny.

*Lights.*

— End of Act II —

\* \* \* \* \*

# ACT III
## SCENE 1


SNOWY
What are you doing?


BEAR
I heard you leave. I followed.


SNOWY
To ruin our fun.


BEAR
Danny.


SNOWY
Go away.
We don't want you here.


BEAR
Danny.


BABS
What is this thing?


GEORGE
This
Old thing's no concern
Of yours or of ours.

Get lost!
Go back down below.

            BEAR
I have the right to
Be here.

            SNOWY
    You lost your rights long
Ago. Go back to
Your box and rot there.

            DANNY
That's not very nice.

            BEAR
Danny.

            SNOWY
    She's not here to help.

            GEORGE
She's not here to play.

I remember this
One — not as well as Snowy,
But I remember.

Take her away, Joe.
Take her to the stairs and cast
Her to the basement.

            BEAR
Danny.

BABS
She scares me.

SNOWY
As well she should.

BEAR
Danny.

SNOWY
Do
Not listen to her.

JOE
Should we be scared of
This walking dishrag?

COUNT
She does
Not scare me.

SNOWY
She should,

For she is not one
Of us. She keeps to herself.

BABS
I think I've heard her.

RECTOR
Is it she who whimpers and
Whines in the blankets
That are piled in the
Corner?

SNOWY
   Alone, for she will
Not join in our games.

GEORGE
She has never joined.
She pines for days before these
Adventures, these games.

SNOWY
She is not welcome
In our sport.

BEAR
   I do not want
To play in your games

GEORGE
She deigns speak with us.

SNOWY
It's no honor sought by us
Nor even welcomed.

BEAR
Unkind words

SNOWY
To an
Unkind Bear.


BEAR
I have done naught
To you, Snowy, nor
To you, George. The rest
I know by sound and laugh and
By reputation,
Though I fear that you
Know me not.


SNOWY
And do not want
To. Our place is here.

Go back below, Bear.
This is no place for you. We
Play, seek life, seek fun.


BEAR
I am not here for
Games or sport.


SNOWY
Again, then, this
Is no place for you.


GEORGE
Danny, bid her go.
The sun still sleeps. We have time
For more adventures.

JOE
I want to be a
Knight, to rescue a damsel
From a fierce dragon.

GEORGE
I'll be the dragon.
I'll take you this time, Sir Knight.
Hmm. Roasted man meat.

RECTOR
Why can't I be the
Dragon?

JOE
You'll be my faithful
Hound.

RECTOR
I'll gladly die
To defend you, my
Master.

JOE
You may have to.

RECTOR
All
Right, then! Let us quest!

COUNT
You'll ne'er catch him, fools,
For his partner is a great
Wizard, master of

Dark and vile magicks,
Costly learned over years of
Apprenticeship in
Transylvania.

Many peasants perished so
I could hone my skills.
Now, I, master and
Count, will help the dragon slay
The forces of good
And bring about the
Dawn of a new era of
Wicked evilness.

### GEORGE
Come, Count, and let us
Vanquish these soft fools. Then we
Can eat the damsel.

### JOE
Fools! This great knight

### RECTOR
And
His heroic hound

### JOE
Will not
Be cowed! Now, we fight!

*Nothing.*

We fight!

RECTOR
We attack.

*Nothing.*

COUNT
Forward, dragon! Beware my
Fireball!

GEORGE
We attack!

*Nothing.*

We strike back!

*Nothing.*

Danny!
Come on! There's a great battle.

GEORGE
Don't leave us hanging.

BEAR
Danny!

SNOWY
Away, Bear!

BABS
Why do I have to be the
Damsel, yet again?
Cannot I be a

Race-car driver? That sounds fun!
I could speed through the
Winding roads of France,
Over snow-capped mountains or
'Cross a vast desert,
The wind whipping through
My hair, sand and sun blinding
Me, but on I drive.

Gas up the car and
Let me go! Please just let me
Turn the ignition.

*Nothing.*

Or let me rescue
Joe, for once. I was Special
Ops, for God's sake.

*Nothing.*

Please!

  BEAR
Danny.

  DANNY
Who…?

  SNOWY
Leave him
Be.

BEAR
Danny.

DANNY
Who…?

SNOWY
There's enough
Time for us to play.

BEAR
You have played enough.

DANNY
Who…?

BEAR
It is time for sleep now.

GEORGE
No. Not sleep. More play.

SNOWY
We should have been more
Silent when we came up. She
Would not have heard us.

BEAR
I have been waiting
For you to come here.

JOE
So you
Could follow us, eh?

BEAR
So I would not have
To go back down alone.

BABS
What
Does that even mean?

SNOWY
Let Babs drive her car.
Let George be a wild dragon.
Then we'll bounce again.

JOE
I could bounce again.

BABS
Not for a while, you can't.

JOE
Hey!

SNOWY
We are here for you.
Danny. Remember
All the games, the adventures.
That is all we want.

We can even play
A diff'rent time, a diff'rent
Place, every night.

BEAR
It is time for bed..

SNOWY

No!

GEORGE
   You can sleep when the sun
Is out. It is night.
The moon gives enough
Light. Your keeper is upstairs.
There's naught to stop us.

JOE
I haven't shown you
My kung-fu grip.

RECTOR
   I can do
Cartwheels! With one hand!

BABS
I bought a red sports
Car. I can drive faster than
Any man.

JOE
   Can not!

COUNT
I'll clean all the blood
From my castle.

SNOWY
   Please, Danny.
Do not go to sleep.

BEAR
It is time for bed.

SNOWY
No!

BEAR
Danny.

GEORGE
And I say 'no!'
We outnumber you.

SNOWY
It's democratic.
We six say you go.

GEORGE
You go.

BEAR
I —

JOE
They said go!

BABS
Go!

DANNY
Stop.

SNOWY
Danny!

DANNY

I said,
'Stop'. I know these. I know them.
Friends of my childhood.

I do not know you.

SNOWY

He does not know her! Hooray!
Away, Bear.

GEORGE

Get lost.

BEAR

He does know me.

SNOWY

He
Said 'not'. Listen to the man.
We'll play with the boy.

Danny, I taught you
So much. We've had so many
Adventures, wars, quests.

We taught you to dream.
We took you to times, places,
You could ne'er visit.

We opened your mind
To limitless games and fun.
We gave you childhood.

BEAR
That's all well and good.

SNOWY
It was what he needed. It
Was what we gave him.

What did you e'er give,
Mangy and molding? What could
You give from a box
Of dusty rags in
A forgotten corner, to
A child who forgot

You? I'm the oldest.

BEAR
Barely old enough to be
Young.

SNOWY
I was the first.

BEAR
Far from first. Not too
Old.

GEORGE
Can you give him what we
Did? A life of joy?
A life of carefree
Fun and endless games?

BEAR
No.

GEORGE
Then.

BEAR
But I could, did, once.

COUNT
Can you turn his bed
Into a spaceship?

RECTOR
Can you
Make this room a sea?

SNOWY
He owes us so much.
We taught him how to dream. You?

BEAR
I taught him to sleep.

\* \* \* \* \*

# ACT III
## SCENE 2


BEAR
I taught him to sleep,
For sleep is where dreams are found.
Remember, Danny?

No. You would...could...not.
I was almost as big as
You, then. Long ago.

I listened as your
Mother sang soft and gentle
Lullabies. Then, as
You slept, I sang them
To keep your eyes closed and you
Safe in slumber's arms.

Don't you remember?

DANNY
I recall my mother's voice —
So long, long ago.

I recall not her
Songs, for I did not care for
Such childish things, I.

I wanted to play
And gallop and to seek strange
And exciting worlds.

BEAR

And I was even
Old and worn by then, and you
Replaced me with them.

It was not your fault,
My darling. You had such a
Full life that many
Things, older and tired,
Had to make way for the new,
More interesting.

Yet, when I was moved,
Nay, taken from your arms, you
Yelled and fought and cried,
Until your new friends
Took their places in your arms,
In your life, your fun.

I heard you, though. You
Called for me, and I, in my
Box, could but listen.

I heard your sport, as
You explored your new worlds, arm
In arm with new friends.

I wept, all alone,
At my loss, darling, and wept
Again when new friends

Were banished, replaced
By newer friends. I waited,
Swallowing the tears
My pain and theirs brought.
Someday, I knew, I'd return.
I'd mount, finally,
Those forbidding stairs,
Make my way to near-forgot
Rooms, and come to you.

Now I find that you
Have forgotten.

### DANNY
Forgotten
Much. But those were days...
Very long ago...
Before memory.

I knew
But Mother.

### BEAR
And Bear.

You knew Bear then. I
Slept in your arms. I kept the
Dark and cold away.

I whispered stories,
Sang lullabies, and caressed
You in the darkness.

DANNY
What stories did you
Tell? What songs did you sing? Can
You help me recall.

I see a bear much
Loved.

BEAR
    I was once much plumper.

DANNY
Long since cast away.

BEAR
Nay, not cast, darling
Boy, but taken. You could not
Cast what you so loved.

SNOWY
What games did you play?

GEORGE
What dungeons did you explore?

JOE
What foes did you slay?

BEAR
We would play games as
Soft as rocking in the night.

We would stare out the
Window and see stars
And reach out for them.

    We'd laugh
At the weird shadows
That hid in corners
Just beyond our crib.

    We would
Lie and listen for
Your mother's step...her
Voice. We would wait for her smile
And rejoice in it.

We would lie in our
Bed and plot and plan ways to
Escape our prison
And to explore the
Glorious world we could see
But not yet enter.

    DANNY
The old and young
Are alike — consigned to our
Beds and forced to watch
The world without the
Confines of their small spaces.Sometimes I wonder
If this small room is
All there is. When the door's shut,
Is there naught outside?
Or is it merely
An emptiness?

I fear that
The next time I leave
This bed, I will be
Doomed, condemned, to find out.

#### BEAR
When
You were young, you longed
To take your first steps.

#### DANNY
I fear I've taken my last.
I can't remember
My first.

#### BEAR
I can, my
Darling Danny. Together
We stumbled on all
Fours, bumping, crying.
Soon we were experts at it,
Zooming from this side
'Cross to the other.
So many bruiséd knees.

You
Held me in your teeth.

This wonderful place,
This wonderful room. It was
Our own private world.

We would crawl and roll
And laugh. Great peals were ne'er far
From your tiny lips.


       DANNY
I had not laughed for
Many months before this night.


       BEAR
Laugh for me again,
Darling. Remember
The joy that we once shared. Take
My hand. Leave the bed.


       DANNY
Leave this bed? It has
Been my home, prison. I fear
'T'will be my coffin.


       BEAR
One hand in mine, the
Other holding to the rail,
To chair, sofa, desk,
We trekked down unknown
Paths, revealing brand new worlds.
We were so tall. You,
My darling, were tall
And fierce and proud, and I...I
Cushioned ev'ry fall.

Then came that great day.
I waited with your loving
Mommy and Daddy,
Held open my arms,
And you let go the bed and
Took those brave first steps.

How we crowed that day.
So oft we repeated the
Great feat for neighbors

Friends and family
That by your bedtime you were
Tired and most cranky.

### DANNY

How can anyone
Recall those days. They live but
In memory's fog.

### BEAR

I remember. I.
P'rhaps I am the only one,
But I remember.

### DANNY

I wish I could. They
Sound like wonderful days, but
I cannot see them.

### BEAR

Danny.

DANNY
Yes.

BEAR
Come to
Me.

DANNY
You are too far away.

BEAR
Darling. Come. To. Me.

DANNY
Snowy, bring me my
Walker.

BEAR
Nay, Snowy. Nor cane
Nor walker. Come. Come.

Place your feet upon
The floor, which you have crossed so
Many times, and walk.

DANNY
I cannot!

BEAR
You must!
Be prisoner no longer
To youth nor to age.

The floor is yours. The
Room is yours. The world is yours.
Now, my darling, walk!

My arms are just a
Few steps away. It starts with
One step. Just one step.

        *DANNY hesitantly takes a step.*

      DANNY
Did you see that?

      SNOWY
  I
Did.

      JOE
I've got you, Danny.

      BEAR
  Let
Him do it alone.

      DANNY
I will fall.

      BEAR
  Then fall.
I will catch you.

      BABS
Go, Danny!

DANNY
Look! Look at me! Look
Mommy! I'm walking!

BEAR
My darling, clever,
Brilliant boy! So brave! Step! Walk!
Explore your domains.
You are master here.
Nor age nor nurse can hinder
You.

Take up your sword.

*DANNY grabs a 'sword'.*

Smite down your foes, boy!

*DANNY 'strikes' away.*

SNOWY
Arrgh!

GEORGE
He got me.

RECTOR
Strike me!

COUNT
Blah!

BEAR
You are the master!

DANNY
Can I skip?

BEAR
   Try it!

>       *DANNY skips.*
>       *They all skip.*

SNOWY
Can you hop?

>       *DANNY hops.*

Hop like you have
Never hopped before!

>           *They all hop.*

JOE
Can you run, Danny?

>           *They all run.*
>           *Soon they are running and throwing pillows and laughing gaily.*

BABS
You can't catch me!

COUNT
   I'll get you!

JOE
Hoo-raa!

RECTOR
Come get me!

BEAR
Now, Danny. Can you
Dance?

DANNY
Dance?

BEAR
Dance.

JOE
Incredible!

BEAR
Move with the music.

*They begin to dance slowly.*
*The others hum a soft tune or drum a gentle rhythm.*
*As the toys cheer him on, DANNY dances with each of them.*
*Each dance is different.*
*With SNOWY, the dance is a mix of polka and bouncing.*
*GEORGE and DANNY swing each other around, going faster and faster until*
*GEORGE is finally forced to give up.*
*COUNT and DANNY's dance is swirling capes and flitting mountain mist.*
*JOE dances with stomps and grunts. Together, they resemble beasts sparring in the*
*forest.*

RECTOR
Cossachok!

*He breaks into a wild cossachok.*

*The others simply look at him.*

DANNY
Maybe
Next time.

BABS
You haven't danced with
Me yet, Sir Danny.

*Her dance is, perhaps, more sensual than the other toys are used to. It is also, perhaps, more sensual than DANNY was expecting, but he follows her lead.*

I did learn some things
From Sally ere you kidnapped
Me.

JOE
Rescued.

BABS
(*With a resigned sigh*)
Rescued.

BEAR
You end the dance with
Me. I danced with you first. I
Will dance with you last.

Soft, Danny. Listen
To the gentle music sung
By the dying Moon.

*They Dance.*
*DANNY's energy begins to flag.*
*Arm in arm, BEAR and DANNY sit on the floor.*

It is time to sleep
My darling. To rest with your
Friends and memories.

* * * * *

# ACT III
## SCENE 3


DANNY
I do remember.
I think. I must. For the Moon
Is familiar
As is the feel of
Your arms about me.

    You were…
You were always there.
Yet I forgot you.

You were my last sight ere I'd
Sleep. You were my first
Kiss ev'ry morning.
Yet I forgot you.

    You were
My first love, yet I

Forgot you.

    Are there
Other friends, other loves from
My childhood that I
Forgot?

    George, Snowy,
You were my fast friends for years,

Before the others
Joined in our games. Now,
Our adventures are vivid,
Like they just happened.

Yet, I'd forgotten.

Why would you return to one
Whose fragile love was
So eas'ly forgot?

Have I so little love to
Give that new love needs
Cast out the old?

    I
Merit not your affection.

I had other friends,
Companions in my
Sport. I have forgotten them,
Though they must have been.
Do they live below
With you? Are they now gone, not
Even memories
Of them to remain?

Tell me, love, how many have
I abandoned? Who

Have I have forgot? What
Friends have I hurt?

I know — I
Recall — how I hurt,
How I wept when you
Were sent away.

    I, though, went
On to new friends, new
Loves, new adventures.
So distracted was I by
Education, by
Jobs, first kisses, the
Laughter of a newborn babe,
That I forgot what

Came before. I did
Not, could not, know that while I
Welcomed, embraced, the
New, the old would be
But objects gathering dust
In a forgotten
Corner of a place
I ne'er visited or thought
Of.

    Had you but called
Out to me, perhaps
I would have taken you up
And embraced you, placed...
Honored you in my
Home and remembered the life
We together'd shared.

P'rhaps, though, I would not.
Age steals from us so much that
Was the joy of youth.

Progress always comes
With a price: the loss of so
Much that we held dear.

Must new values e'er
Bury the old? Are our new
Truths inherently
Better than the old?
Must we love by no longer
Loving what we loved?

Did I not have love
Enough to share?

   I loved wife.
I loved my children.

I loved them and I
Remember them. Could I not
Love and remember
You and all my loves?

Snowy, so happy and gay;
Mysterious Count,
So wise in mystic
Ways; wild and proud George; Rector,
Wond'rous Russian hound;
Brave Joe, ready to
Face the fiercest of foes; and
Poor, lost, lov'ly Babs.

So many times did
We set out on epic quests.
Yet, those I forgot.

I remember son's
First steps. I can still weep for
Daughter's first lost crush.
Those moments are clear,
Frozen in time. But moments
That made me the man
I became, I am,
I wish that I were. Those...those
Are long forgotten.

My first laugh is but
An echo lost among time's
Deafening noises.

My first step is a
Faded photograph, molding
In some unknown place.

My first loves, consigned
To boxes and to mem'ries
Lost. I owe you more!

Oh, I am sorry
For my failure. I'm sorry.
Sorry I forgot.

Sorry I could not
Be the boy you remembered,
The boy you risked so

Much to come and find,
Once more to embrace and to
Frolic and play with.

I am sorry most
To you, Bear. Your embrace was
Always as strong and
Secure as from the
Arms of a loving father.
Your sigh, your kiss, your
Gentle voice, your soft
Laugh were perfect, as if from
A baby's mother.

I wish…. Oh, I wish
I had kept you. Kept you all!

I wish I'd given
You to my children
And to theirs, so you and they
Could have shared our joy.

I wish I had braved
The dusty boxes and brought
You back to my life.

I wish I could e'er
Play and run and dream with you.
I know I cannot.

My limbs no longer
Have strength; my falt'ring breath no
Longer has the time.
I must sit and rest

A while. P'rhaps when my breath comes
Back, we can play more.

     BEAR
No, my darling. Now
Is time to shrug off cares and
Woes and close your eyes.

     DANNY
No!

     BEAR
  Yes, darling. Sleep.

     DANNY
No!

     BEAR
  Yes, my love, and rest in
Dearest friends' embrace.

*They all huddle around DANNY.*

\* \* \* \* \*

# ACT III
## SCENE 4


SNOWY

So many times we
Went to my planet to bounce.
So many times. I
Wish we'd stayed. There is
So much I could have shown you.
So many places.
We could have gone to
Other glades, other pastures —
If we'd had the time.

Should I have come?

    Should
I have dared the stairs sooner?

What would I have found?

Who would I have found?

I knew the little boy was
Gone. What of the man?

That is what I feared:
A man so caught up in his
Life that he might no
Longer care for us.
That is what kept me below.

We all forget. Yes.
I have forgot much,
So many friends are just a
Haze in my mem'ries.

That you'd forgot us
Hurt. However, there was so
Much life, so much past,
You had to have lost
Some of it.

I prayed, though, that
Something would come back.
A spark, a hint, would
Remind you of our games.

    We
Could not forget you.

I could not, rather,
For 'tis not my place t'impose
Memories on them.

I could, we did, make
You remember. We could not,
Did not, make you care.

You did care, so for
One brief shining moment, we'd
Make fresh memories.

Take the meadows with
You, Danny boy. Take the glades,
Wherever you go.

RECTOR
I came this close to
Defeating the damned Skelnik
I could have. Would have.

COUNT
Did you ever?

RECTOR
(*Thinks*)
No.

COUNT
If I'd had the maiden's blood —

BABS
Leave me out of this.

COUNT
I could have helped you.
We could have cornered the beast.
I'd have weakened him.

RECTOR
I could have slain him.
What then?

COUNT
What?

RECTOR
After such a
Great victory? What?

COUNT
I don't know. Are there
Not other fell beasts roaming
Siberian steppes?

RECTOR
Not that I've heard of.

COUNT
You could then join with me in
Transylvania.

RECTOR
What is there?

COUNT
Where?

RECTOR
In
Transylvania!?

COUNT
Werewolves.

RECTOR
I do not know where.

COUNT
Maidens to devour.

BABS
Leave me out of this.

RECTOR
Is there
Anything else?

COUNT
(*Thinks*)
Trees.

RECTOR
Trees?

COUNT
A lot of trees.
All over the place. Had to
Fly among the trees.

RECTOR
Because of the dark.

COUNT
The dark?

RECTOR
In the night, for you
Vampires fear the Sun.

COUNT
We don't fear Sun. That
Is a myth. Myth!

BABS
I said, leave
Me out of this.

JOE
Babs.


BABS
It was a red sports
Car. Red. Sports. Car. Expensive.
JOE
How much did it cost?


BABS
A lot.


JOE
Wow! That much!


COUNT
Danny made me be afraid
Of the Sun because
He was afraid I
Would have too much power.


RECTOR
That
Makes a lot of sense.


COUNT
Like the whole mirror
Thing.


BABS
It was a beautiful
Car. Very dashing.

COUNT
I look good in a
Mirror. Very regal.

RECTOR
But
You are not a king.

COUNT
Then I look ducal.

RECTOR
Yet, you are nor a duke, Count.

COUNT
Countal?

RECTOR
That does not
Sound right.

BABS
It was fast.
Faster than any tank.

JOE
I
Wish I'd driven it.

BABS
You did.

JOE
I did?

BABS
    You
Did — drove it off the landing,
Tot'lling it downstairs.

RECTOR
What's a count?

COUNT
    Four or
Five pounds?

RECTOR
    (*After a song silent groan*)
    Are you many?

COUNT
    (*Smugly*)
We're
Very numerate.

JOE
I was attacking
The Russian Army.

BABS
    In my
Sports car.

JOE
Red. Sports. Car.

BABS
Your point?

JOE
Camouflage.

BABS
Camouflage?

JOE
Of course. It was
The Russian Army.

BABS and RECTOR
You're an idiot.

JOE and COUNT
Hey!

RECTOR
Shut up, Count.

BABS
Why attack
The Russian Army?

JOE
They had kidnapped you.

BABS
Why does everyone want
To kidnap me? Why?

Astronaut. Model.
Power broker. I should have
Been an accountant.

Accountants are so
Excruciatingly dull.
That's it! I am one!
No one kidnaps the
Accountant!

          JOE
     Then I would have
No one to rescue.

          GEORGE
Snowy. Do you think
We could have a jungle in
The basement? Not a
Large one, mind you, but
One we could swing on. From time
To time. Just for fun.

We could have vines that
Would take us to Count's castle
Or to the ice caves
Of Siberia,
With a stopover at Bab's
Penthouse, where we could
Watch Joe storm beaches
While we bounced. We could do that,
Snowy. Couldn't we?

          SNOWY
I do not know, George,
Though I fear, 'no'. We have had
Our last adventure.

BEAR
Rest now, friends. Lie down
And bring warming embraces
To our sleeping love.

# ACT III
## SCENE 5

BEAR
Feel their arms about
You and know undying love.
Sleep, my darling, sleep.

There's more than enough
Love for all loves, for friends both
Old and new. There is
Love enough to warm
All their hearts and comfort yours.

Their love will not fade
And will ever be
With you, wherever you go,
What journeys you take.

You may have forgot,
But that is the fate of all
Joy: to wither, fade.

We lived for you, in
Your hopes and your dreams. Nothing
Can take that from us,
Though, perhaps, it is
That same nothing that will take
Us at last from you.

Our time stopped when you
Let us go. As painful as
That was, we all knew
That time would come. You
Had to grow, to move on, to
Find new friends, new loves.

As much as we missed
Your laughter and your games, we
Rejoiced in your life.

There is so much love
From those who embrace you. So
Much from you to them.

*BEAR looks at the lying figures.*

Where's the love for Bear?
Was it just that brief moment
Between your first cries
And your adventures
Conqu'ring lands and stealing hearts?
Was I e'er needed,
Or was I merely
A prop to be cast off ere
The end of act one?

Where's the love for Bear?
Where are the kisses, the hugs
That I've so longed for?

Oft I feared that I
Would forget, that the mem'ries
Would fly far away.

Then I would hear your
Laugh, see smile, taste tears, recall
Mother's lullaby.

> BEAR *sings in a chanting way.*
> *The tune is not important, though there is one.*

Come, darling.
Come to bed.
Lay your head upon the clouds
And let the wind rock you
In the limbs of a rainbow tree.

See the smiling moon
Soar into the sky.
We will play again tomorrow,
When the sun is high.

Day is short.
Light is gone.
There is little laughter left.
Hold tight to those you love
Sleep in the arms of those who care.

See the smiling moon
Soar into the sky.
We will play again tomorrow,
When the sun is high.

Games are done.
Eyes are closed.
Breathe the sweet air one last time.
Feel the loving warmth, dear,
As we still hold you in our arms.

See the smiling moon
Soar into the sky.
We will play again tomorrow,
When the sun is high.

Lie, darling.
Stay in bed.
You head rests upon the clouds.
The winds will now take you
On your great last adventure, dear.

Oh, the weeping Moon
Set's into the earth.
We'll not play tomorrow,
For the sun won't rise.

> *The toys kiss DANNY and leave, until only BEAR and DANNY remain.*

We will be taken
On our last journeys as well.
We will not know where.
Perhaps we will be
Together, somehow. Somehow.
Then we'll remember,
If that be our fate.
We'll remember and relive
All of our great games.

I wish...we all wish,
That we could join you and guide
You and comfort you.

I, perhaps, more than
The others, for I was first.
I was your first love.

No one understands
Why I adore you. Yet, I
Dream your soft kisses.
No one understands
Why I need you. Yet you are
The breath that fills me.
No one understands
Why I love you. But, without
You, there are no dreams.
Without you, there are
No kisses or breath. Without
You, there is no point.

There's the love for Bear.
Given to you from your first
Love, to her last love.

## *End.*

\* \* \* \* \*

# *Director/Playwright's Note*

A few years ago, my son and I were playing with his toys when he asked me if he would still love his toys when he got older. I said that I certainly hoped he would and that I still loved many of my old toys — though the relationships have changed somewhat over the years. Then Christopher asked a harder question: "Will they still love me?" I did not ask Christopher the even harder question: "Should they?" I thought about it a lot, though. I did not come up with an answer, but I did come up with FIRST LOVE, LAST LOVE.

## *Original Production Cast & Crew*

The play was performed by the Needham Community Theatre in a digital streaming production presented in October of 2020.

# CAST:

Snowy (stuffed bunny):  Ilan Barzilay
Rector (stuffed dog):  Joel Hersh
Count (stuffed vampire):  Joe Lanctot
George (stuffed monkey):  Matthew R. Divoll
Joe (action figure):  Alex Slocum
Babs (fashion doll):  Tessa Tropeano
Danny (old man):  Michael Bailit
Bear (stuffed bear):  Marianne Phinney

# CREW:

Playwright/Director:  Edward Eaton
Producer:  Nicki Ramshaw
Stage Manager/Sound:  Eva Taub
Tech Coordinator:  Dan Henderson
Tech Coordinator:  Chris Tess

\* \* \* \* \*

# ABOUT THE AUTHOR

Edward Eaton has studied and taught in the States, China, Israel, Oman, and France. He holds a PhD in Theatre History and Literature. With a background in playwriting, he has worked as a theater director and fight choreographer, a newspaper columnist, and a theater critic. An avid SCUBA diver and skier, he resides in Massachusetts with his wife Silviya and son Christopher.

\* \* \* \* \*